Church of the Holy Sepulchre

Western Wall

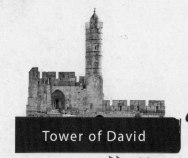

Tower of David

Cardo

Dome of the Rock

Hezekiah's Tunnel

Montefiore Windmill

Journey through Jerusalem

By Amanda Benjamin

Illustrated by Tamar Blumenfeld

Springfield, NJ • Jerusalem

For the real Mirri, Jem, Olivia and Bex
and
for Dror

We would like to thank those who kindly shared their time and knowledge with us:
Judy Goldman, the Right Reverend Kirk Stevan Smith and Rabbi Kerry M. Olitzky

The publisher wishes to credit the following photographs:
Shutterstock: p. 3, Bridge of Strings: Evgeny Beloshabsky; pp. 5-6, Montefiore Windmill: Arkady Mazor; pp. 6-7, Old City: S1001; p. 7, Hezekiah's Tunnel: Robert Hoetink; cover/pp. 8-9, Old City walls: Sean Pavone; p. 10, Jaffa Gate entrance: Fotokon2; p. 11, Cardo: Flik47; p. 14, Via Dolorosa: Anton Ivanov, Via Dolorosa sign: Ilia Torlin; p. 18, bread: Seregalsv; p. 19, Machane Yehuda Market: ChameleonsEye3 & 4; p. 21, Knesset: Irina Opachevsky; p. 22, Shrine of the Book: Matthew Delaney. Other sources: p. 15, spice store: Barry Hotchkies/Behrman House photo contest; p. 16, Church of the Holy Sepulchre: Noam Chen/Israeli Ministry of Tourism www.goisrael.com; pp. 17-18, light rail: Wikimedia Commons/Leinad; p. 20, Rehavia villa: Wikimedia Commons/sir kiss; p. 23, Second Temple Model: Wikimedia Commons; p. 24, Jerusalem Forest: Wikimedia Commons/Dror Feitelson; back cover, Western Wall: Alberto Peral.

Back cover quote from *A Beggar in Jerusalem* by Elie Wiesel. Copyright © 1970 by Elie Wiesel. Used by permission of Georges Borchardt, Inc., on behalf of Elirion Associates, Inc.

Apples & Honey Press
An imprint of Behrman House and Gefen Publishing House
Behrman House, 11 Edison Place, Springfield, New Jersey 07081
Gefen Publishing House Ltd., 6 Hatzvi Street, Jerusalem 94386, Israel
www.applesandhoneypress.com

Copyright © 2017 Apples & Honey Press

ISBN 978-1-68115-531-9

Library of Congress Cataloging-in-Publication Data

Names: Benjamin, Amanda, author. | Blumenfeld, Tamar, illustrator.
Title: Journey through Jerusalem / by Amanda Benjamin ; illustrations by Tamar Blumenfeld.
Description: Springfield, New Jersey : Apples & Honey Press, 2017. | Summary: A mother cat and her three kittens travel to Jerusalem, seeing the city's iconic structures presented through a combination of photographic and illustrative elements.
Identifiers: LCCN 2016032020 | ISBN 9781681155319
Subjects: | CYAC: Jerusalem--Fiction. | Cats--Fiction. | Jews--Fiction.
Classification: LCC PZ7.1.B4533 Jo 2017 | DDC [E]--dc23 LC record available at https://lccn.loc.gov/2016032020

Design by Alexandra N. Segal
Printed in China
2 4 6 8 10 9 7 5 3 1

"Hush, kittens," soothed Olivia, their mother. "We're just being taken out for the day. I was born here in Jerusalem, you know!"

The truck crunched to a halt, and Mirri poked her head out of the basket.

"MAMA, is that a windmill over there?" she gasped.

"Don't even think about—!" Olivia warned.

"MIRRI...!"

It was too late! One...two...three kittens had jumped out. With a soft thud, Olivia landed on the sidewalk next to them, as the truck disappeared around a bend.

"COME ON,"
called Mirri.
"Let's climb that windmill!"

"But first—how about a visit to Hezekiah's Tunnel?"

Soon the cats arrived at the famous underground tunnels, just outside the Old City.

"Who wants to go and explore?" asked Olivia.

"WE DO!" three little voices cried.

"Ew, Ew, Ew!"
squeaked Bex.
"There's water down here!"

"That was fun!" called Mirri.
"What's next?"

"The Old City!
Come on, everyone!"

"Mama," whispered Bex, as they trotted along the great stone walls toward the Tower of David. "How will we find our way home?"

"Oh, sweetie, don't worry!" said Olivia.

"We cats have a purr-fect sense of direction."

"The Jaffa Gate entrance into the city will be full of people," Olivia told her kittens, "so everyone stick together."

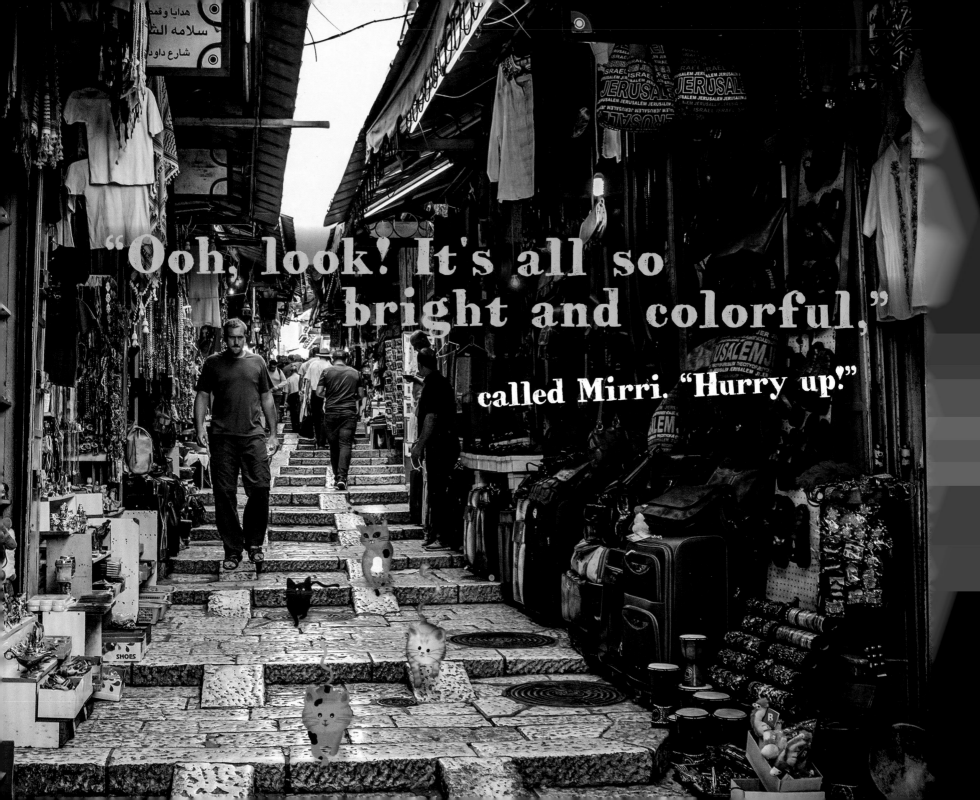

"Ooh, look! It's all so bright and colorful," called Mirri. "Hurry up!"

"The Western Wall of an ancient Temple."
"What are these pieces of paper stuck in between the stones?" asked Mirri.
"They are very precious notes written to God. People come from all over the world to put them here. Come on!"

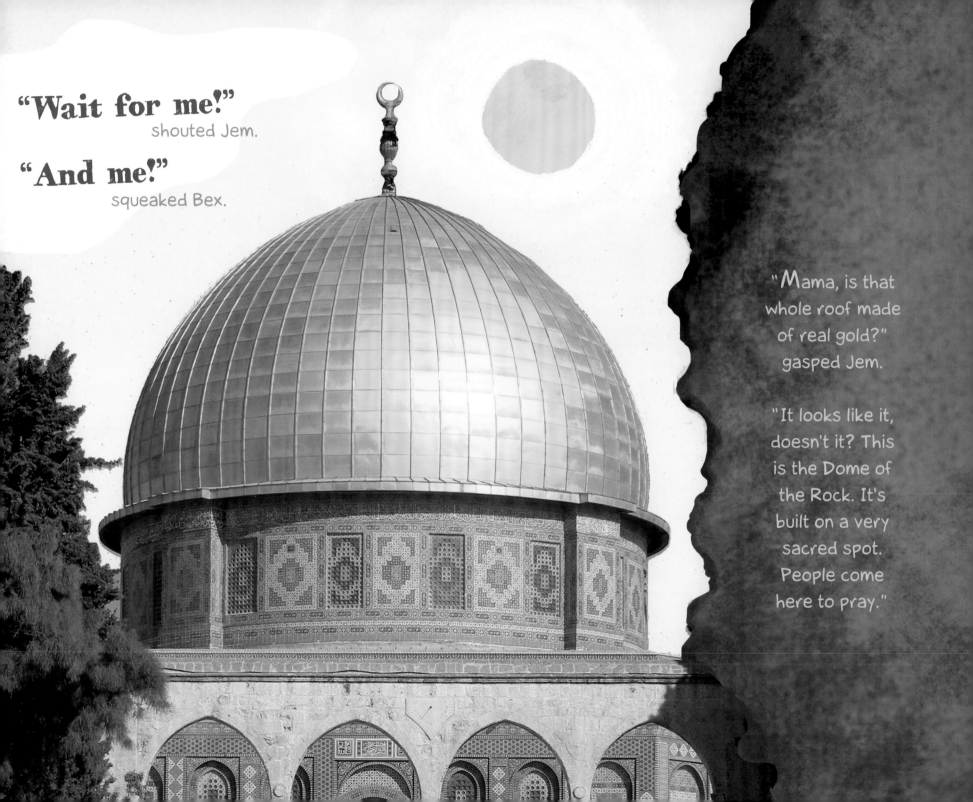

"Wait for me!" shouted Jem.

"And me!" squeaked Bex.

"Mama, is that whole roof made of real gold?" gasped Jem.

"It looks like it, doesn't it? This is the Dome of the Rock. It's built on a very sacred spot. People come here to pray."

"Wow, look. Cool!" said Jem. "That's what we just saw. A wooden model of the Dome of the Rock."
"What's that, up ahead?" called Mirri.

"Ahh," answered Olivia. "That's the Church of the Holy Sepulchre. People come here to pray too, and light candles to remind us of all the miracles in the world."

"I'm hungry!" said Bex.

Soon, four hungry cats were licking their lips at the Mahane Yehuda Market.
  "Mama," purred Bex happily, "this has been the best day ever!
Where are we going next?"

A little way from the market, they saw two people on bicycles.
"Let's get a ride," whispered Olivia.
Olivia and Bex jumped into one basket...

while Mirri and
Jem snuggled
comfortably
into the other.

They stopped at a big building with blue and white flags outside. The cats jumped out.

"Thanks for the ride," they meowed.
"What is this place?" Mirri asked her mother curiously.
"It's the Knesset. Where all the important laws are made," answered Olivia. "You see, Jerusalem is the capital of Israel. There's one more place not far from here I want to show you."

"Mama, that's just a giant beehive!"

Olivia smiled. "No, there are no bees in there! That's the Shrine of
the Book, the special home of the oldest Hebrew Bible ever found."
"Why is water squirting onto it?" asked Jem.
"To keep it cool, even in the hottest weather," his mother explained.

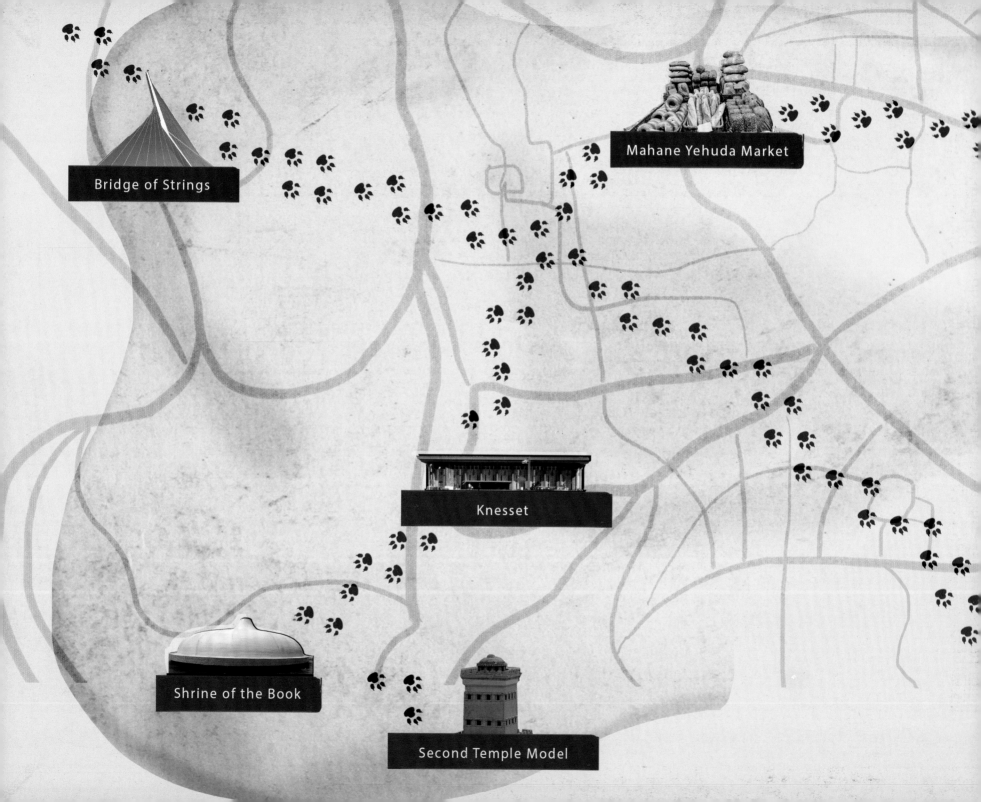

Bridge of Strings

Mahane Yehuda Market

Knesset

Shrine of the Book

Second Temple Model